Tom and Ricky

and the

Siamese Turtle Mystery

Bob Wright

High Noon Books

Novato, California

The Siamese Turtle Mystery

Bob Wright
AR B.L.: 2.4
Points: 0.5   UG

Cover Design: Nancy Peach
Interior Illustrations: Herb Heidinger

International Standard Book Number: 0-87879-330-5

9 8 7 6 5 4
20 19

You'll enjoy all the High Noon Books. Write for
a free full list of titles.

Contents

CHAPTER 1

The Rock Garden

"Tom! Tom!" Ricky called. "Come on over."

Ricky was in his back yard.

"What are you doing?" Tom said. He got off his dirt bike.

"I have to help my mom," Ricky said. "We're cleaning the yard."

Patches, Ricky's dog, saw Tom. Patches didn't move. He just wagged his tail.

"My mom wants to plant some tomatoes. I'm picking out the rocks," Ricky said.

"Can I help?" Tom said. "I don't have anything to do today."

"Sure. Help me get rocks. We can put all of them right here," Ricky said.

Tom picked up rocks. Patches didn't move. He watched Tom and Ricky. Patches kept one eye open. The other was closed.

"What are you going to do with all the rocks?" Tom asked.

"I'm going to fix them up. Then I'm going to buy some turtles," Ricky said.

"Hey! You could make a place for them to swim around," Tom said.

Tom and Ricky had enough rocks now. They put them into a circle. They dug a hole.

2

"It looks good," Tom said.

"Wait a minute. I'll get a pan from my mom. We can put a big pan in that hole. That way the water won't run out," Ricky said.

Ricky ran into the house. Then he came back with a big pan. He put it in the hole. Then he got the hose. He filled the pan.

"Hey! Why don't we make a waterfall?" Tom said.

They put the hose up on some big rocks. The water ran down into the pan.

"This looks great!" Tom said.

"Yeah. Now we need to get some turtles," Ricky said.

Ricky's mom came into the yard.

3

"Ricky, that looks good. But you can't leave the water on. Everything will be muddy. The water is going out of the pan," she said.

Patches started to step into the pan.

"Patches! Stay out of there," Ricky said.

Patches stepped back.

"Why don't you dig another hole? That way the water can go from the pan to the tomato plants," Ricky's mom said.

The boys made another hole for water. It worked very well. They thought it looked very good, too.

"Now we can get some turtles," Ricky said.

"There's a new pet store. I went by it this morning. I saw turtles in the window," Tom said.

"I have a dollar," Ricky said.

"I have 75 cents," Tom said.

"We need a little more," Ricky said.

*"Hey! Patches. Stay out of there," Ricky said.
Patches stepped back.*

"Here's another dollar for helping to clean the yard," Ricky's mom said.

"That should be enough for a few turtles," Ricky said.

"They'll like it there," Tom said.

"OK. Let's go," Ricky said. He got on his bike. Tom got on his.

When Patches heard "go," he jumped up. He wanted to go with Tom and Ricky.

"All right, Patches. You can come along," Ricky said.

CHAPTER 2

The New Pet Store

The pet store was new. It had just opened. There were lots of people in it. It had many fish and animals for sale.

Tom and Ricky stopped in front of the store. They locked their bikes. Patches went in with them.

A man saw Tom and Ricky and Patches. He looked mad. "What do you want?" he asked.

"We want to buy some turtles," Ricky said.

"I have a large desert turtle," the man said.

"No. We want some of those small turtles," Tom said.

"These are the ones we want to buy," Ricky said. He pointed to the pretty turtles in the window.

"I have never seen turtles like these," Tom said. "Where are they from?"

"Those turtles are from Siam," the man said.

Tom and Ricky kept looking at the turtles. They were very pretty. The shells were tall. They were all different colors.

"How much are they?" Ricky asked.

"Those turtles are not for sale," the man said. "I told you the only turtle for sale is the large one. Now make up your minds," he said.

The man was mad. There were other people in the store. He went to see what they wanted to buy.

"I don't like him," Ricky said.

Patches barked at the man. He didn't like him either.

They kept on looking at the small turtles.

Then a lady saw them looking at the turtles. She walked over to them.

"Hello. I work here. Can I help you with anything?" she said.

We sure like these turtles," Ricky said.

"Yes. I do, too. They are very pretty. Let me find how much they are." She walked over to the man. He was busy with other people.

The lady tried to ask about the turtles. Then she came back.

"Mr. Hall is very busy. But I think they are 25 cents each. Tomorrow they will be one dollar each. We have eleven of them," she said.

"Hey. We have $2.75. We can buy all of them," Ricky said.

"You will need 15 cents for the sales tax," the lady said.

"Can we bring it later?" Ricky asked.

"I think that will be all right," she said.

The lady got a small box. She put all eleven turtles in it.

"Those are the only Siamese turtles we have. Now they are all gone," she said.

They paid the lady. Then they took the box and got on their bikes.

As soon as they got home, they showed Ricky's mom the turtles.

"My, they are very pretty," she said.

They ran into the back yard. Patches ran after them. They put all eleven turtles in the water. Ricky turned the hose on. The turtles seemed to like their new home. They swam in the water. Some climbed out on the rocks.

"I bet they like it there in the water," Ricky said.

"Yeah. They just had rocks to climb on at the store," Tom said.

Even Patches was watching the turtles.

Then Tom called, "Hey! Look! The water. It is turning red and blue and yellow!"

"The color is coming off the turtles," Ricky said.

"Look. The turtles are grey. They were painted. Their real color is grey," Tom said.

"That isn't fair," Ricky said.

"Let's go back to the pet store. We'll ask the lady about this," Tom said.

"Be sure to take the 15 cents we owe her," Ricky said.

They got on their bikes. This time Patches stayed home. He wanted to keep on looking at the turtles.

CHAPTER 3

A Bad Mistake

Tom and Ricky got back to the pet store. The lady saw them when they walked into the store. There were still many people buying pets. But she came over to them.

"Boys, I made a mistake this morning. Those turtles were not for sale. I will need to have them back," she said.

"Why can't you sell them?" Ricky asked.

"Those turtles were not for sale. I made a mistake," she said.

"We brought the 15 cents we owe you," Ricky said.

"And we want to tell you about the turtles. The colors are coming off. Those turtles were painted. Those were not their real colors," Tom said.

"Keep the 15 cents. I will give you your money back. Just bring those turtles back right now." The lady seemed to be getting mad.

Then Mr. Hall came over.

"These are the boys who bought the turtles, Mr. Hall. I told them to bring them back," she said.

"I told you boys those turtles were not for sale," Mr. Hall said.

The lady gave Tom the $2.75. Then she said, "Now go get the turtles."

"I want them right away. Get them or I will call the police," Mr. Hall said.

Tom and Ricky went out to their bikes.

"Boy, are they mad," Ricky said.

When they got home, Ricky's mom had the TV on. It was the news.

"Hey, Mom," Ricky said.

"Wait a minute. The news is almost over," she said.

The man on the TV talked about the weather. Then he said that some rubies had been stolen from the King of Siam. Ricky's mom turned the TV off.

"What's up?" she asked.

"The man at the pet store wants the turtles back. He said they should not have been sold," Ricky said.

"What's wrong with them?" she asked.

"We don't know. They gave us our money back," Tom said.

"Well, you had better take them back," she said.

"I wonder why they couldn't sell them," Tom said.

"Maybe it was because of those colors," Ricky said.

Ricky's mom got the box they came in. They all went to get the turtles.

"You know, Tom, they are very funny looking," Ricky said.

"But they sure looked pretty when we got them," Tom said.

"No. I mean those shells. Turtles have low shells. That makes it easier for them to swim. Those tall shells look funny now that they are grey," Ricky said.

Ricky picked up one of the turtles.

"Hey, Tom. Feel this shell. It is soft. Shells on turtles should be very hard," Ricky said.

Tom touched the shell of the turtle. It was soft.

As Tom was touching the turtle, the top of the shell came off. It was like a little cap.

"Hey, look at this," Ricky said.

Now the turtle looked like other turtles. It had a hard, flat shell.

"What's going on?" Tom asked.

"I don't know. The top of the shell came off," Ricky said.

"What did you do to it?" Tom asked.

"I was just holding it," Ricky said.

"Here. Let me see it," Tom said.

"Wait a minute. I think I see something," Ricky said.

Tom moved closer to Ricky and the turtle.

Tom took the little cap and looked at it. They could see something inside of it. It shined in the sun light.

"Hey. Will you look at that. Look at the way it shines," Tom said.

Ricky tried to see what Tom was holding.

Tom took the little cap and looked at it.
They could see something inside of it.

CHAPTER 4

A Surprise

They looked at the thing that was shining.

"What is it?" Ricky asked.

"I don't know. Let me get a little stick. Something is stuck in there," Tom said. The little thing that was shining wouldn't come out.

"Maybe my mom has something we can use," Ricky said. He put the turtle back in the water. Now it was easy for it to swim.

Tom and Ricky went inside. Ricky's mom was in the kitchen.

"Mom, the top of a turtle shell came off. There is something stuck in the top. Can you get it out?" Ricky asked.

"Let me see what I can do," she said. "It looks like a little piece of glass."

Ricky's mom got a pin. She tried and tried. It wouldn't come out. Then she broke the shell.

The thing that was shining was like a marble. It had many flat sides. Ricky's mom held it up to the light. It made many colors as the sun light went through it.

"It's a marble," Tom said.

"No. This isn't a marble. It is a pretty red stone," she said.

"What about the other turtles?" Ricky asked.

"Maybe they have soft shells, too," he said.

Tom and Ricky ran into the back yard. They were excited. Even Patches started barking.

They picked up all the turtles. They took them into the house. The shells were wet and soft. They had been in the water a long time.

"Put them in the box. That way they won't fall off the table," Ricky's mom said.

"Take the top part off carefully. We don't want to hurt the turtles," Ricky's mom said.

One by one they pulled the soft shells off. Now all the turtles looked the way they should look. Their shells were plain and flat.

"Someone must have put these tops on with very hard glue," Ricky said.

"The water made them soft," Tom said.

"That's why they didn't put the turtles in water at the pet store," Ricky's mom said.

As Tom took the shells off, he gave them to Ricky. Ricky took the red stones out.

Ricky's mom held each one up to the sun light. The light coming through each one made many colors.

"Hey," Ricky said. "We have to take the turtles back to the store. Put them in the box."

They got on their bikes. They were in such a hurry that they forgot the red stones on the table at home.

CHAPTER 5

Strange Visitor

Tom and Ricky walked back into the pet store. Mr. Hall saw them. He also saw the box in Tom's hands. He walked quickly over to them.

"Are all the turtles in the box?" he asked. He tried to sound nice. But Tom and Ricky could see that he was still mad.

"Yes, they are all here. All eleven of them," Ricky said.

"Well. Give them to me. You have your money," he said.

Ricky gave him the box. Then they started to leave.

Mr. Hall opened the box. He yelled, "Wait a minute! Stop! Come back here!"

Tom and Ricky turned around. They walked back to Mr. Hall.

"These aren't my turtles. Where are the ones you bought here?"

"Those are the same turtles," Tom said.

"The paint came off when we put them in water. We're sorry about that," Ricky said.

"And the fake shells came off, too," Tom added.

"Where are the tops? I can paint them again. I want them back," Mr. Hall yelled.

Everyone in the store was looking at Mr. Hall. He stopped for a minute.

"They're at my house," Ricky said.

"We couldn't help it. The shells got soft in the water," Tom said.

Mr. Hall tried to be nice. "Now, boys. These are my turtles. I told you they were not for sale. Now go get those tops!"

"There was something funny about those tops, Mr. Hall," Ricky said. "There were little red stones in them."

"Yeah," Tom added. "And they really look pretty when the sun shines on them."

Just then another man walked into the store.

Mr. Hall kept looking at the strange man.

The man walked over to Mr. Hall.

"I am here for those special turtles. Where are they?" the stranger asked.

"I am here for those special turtles.
Where are they?"

Mr. Hall looked at Tom and Ricky. Then he said to the stranger, "Come with me."

Mr. Hall and the stranger walked into the back room. Tom and Ricky could hear them yelling. They were both mad.

"Shall we go or shall we stay?" Ricky asked.

"I think we better go," Tom said.

Just then Mr. Hall came back into the store. He called to Tom and Ricky.

"Come here for a minute. I want to see you," he said.

The boys went into the back room. The stranger was still there. "Now listen. I don't want any trouble. You took my turtles," he said.

Tom and Ricky just looked at him.

"I don't care what you found in them. I want those tops. Do you hear me?" he said.

"Yes," Tom said.

"Have you told anyone else about the turtles?" the stranger asked.

"Only my mother," Ricky said.

"What did your mother say?" the stranger asked.

"She wondered what those red stones were," Ricky said.

"They are nothing. Just little pieces of glass. They made the turtles look pretty," the stranger said. He smiled at Tom and Ricky. He was trying hard to sound nice.

"Yes, he is right," Mr. Hall said. "They are just red glass."

"Shut up!" the stranger said to Mr. Hall.

Then the stranger turned back to Tom and Ricky. "I will give you each $5.00 if you bring those tops back here right away. But you must go fast or I won't give you the money. Is that clear?"

Both boys said, "Yes!"

"Now go quickly. I will wait for you right here," the stranger said.

Tom and Ricky went out to their bikes.

"I don't like Mr. Hall or that other man," Tom said.

"I don't like any of this," Ricky said.

"What is all this about?" Tom asked.

"I don't know. Let's get out of here as fast as we can," Ricky answered.

They got on their bikes and rode home as fast as they could. They didn't like Mr. Hall and now they didn't like the stranger.

CHAPTER 6

The Police Help Out

Tom and Ricky ran into the house when they got home.

"What's the matter? Slow down," Ricky's mother said.

They told her about the stranger at the pet store. And how he wanted the tops of the turtle shells back. And how he would give them $5.00 each.

"He said the red stones were little pieces of red glass," Tom said.

"That's funny. Then why does he want them?" she asked.

"We don't know. He just said they were his turtles," Ricky said.

"But you gave him back the turtles," she said.

"He said he wanted everything," Tom said.

"I don't like any of this," she said.

"What should we do?" Ricky asked.

"I think you had better call the police. This sounds like trouble to me," she said.

Ricky went to the telephone. He called the police. He told them about buying the turtles, about the colors coming off the turtles, the fake shells, and the red stones they had found.

"Stay right at home," the policeman said.

"I am coming out with someone else to see you. I will be right there."

Ricky phoned the police. He told them about the red stones they found.

Tom and Ricky sat and waited. Then a police car stopped in front of the house. One policeman got out with another man. They came to the front door. Ricky went to open it.

"Are you the one who called us about the turtles?" the policeman asked.

"Yes, I am," answered Ricky.

"May we come in? I am Sergeant Collins. This is Mr. Wells," the policeman said.

Tom and Ricky showed Sergeant Collins the fake shells and the red stones.

Mr. Wells looked at each stone very carefully. Then he said, "Yes, I am sure. These are rubies. They are worth a lot of money."

Tom and Ricky looked at one another.

"Mr. Hall at the pet store said they were Siamese turtles," Ricky said.

"What do you think, Mr. Wells?" Sergeant Collins asked.

"I think these could be the eleven rubies stolen from the King of Siam," he answered.

"If they are, they will be worth a lot of money," Sergeant Collins said.

"What will happen now?" Ricky asked.

"We will have to take these rubies with us," Sergeant Collins said. He gave Ricky a note saying that he had taken the eleven rubies. Ricky put it in his pocket.

"What do we do about Mr. Hall at the pet store?" Tom asked.

"Don't worry about that. We are going down to the pet store right now. We will have a very long talk with Mr. Hall and the stranger," Sergeant Collins said.

"Will we need to go, too?" Ricky asked.

"There is no need for that. We have everything we need," Sergeant Collins said.

"Do you know what this is all about?" Ricky asked.

"We might know," Sergeant Collins said.

"When do you think you will know for sure?" Ricky asked.

"By tomorrow," Sergeant Collins said.

"Will you let us know how everything turns out?" Tom asked.

"We will come by tomorrow and tell you all about it. You were right to call us. We think we have cracked a very important case. You were a great help to us," Sergeant Collins said.

The policeman and the man left.

"I can hardly wait to see what happens," Tom said.

"We'll know tomorrow," Ricky said.

CHAPTER 7

The Case is Solved

The next day Sergeant Collins came by to see Tom and Ricky.

"Everything turned out fine. Mr. Hall and the stranger were waiting for you boys to get back. We surprised them. They are both in jail. We have everything we need to put them away for a long time," Sergeant Collins said.

"What was this all about?" Ricky asked.

"Yeah. What were those rubies doing in the turtles?" Tom asked.

"Wait. Slow down. I'll tell you everything. Mr. Hall used the pet store as a front. He didn't like pets or animals. He had the pet store just to smuggle rubies into the country," Sergeant Collins said.

"What about the stranger?" Ricky asked.

"He was one of the people who was buying rubies from Mr. Hall. A lot of people really wanted to buy pets and animals. But other people were there just to buy turtles with rubies in them," Sergeant Collins answered.

"You mean the only reason he sold turtles was to hide the rubies?" Ricky asked.

"Yes, that is right," Sergeant Collins said.

"What about the lady there?" Tom asked.

"She likes pets. She is going to take over the store," Sergeant Collins said.

"Great! Let's go back and get the turtles for the rock garden," Tom said.

"That's a good idea, if she still sells turtles," Ricky said.

Tom and Ricky were getting ready to leave. Sergeant Collins called out, "Wait. I forgot to tell you. You will get a reward for helping us find those gems. Good luck. Thanks for your help."

"Come on, Tom," Ricky said. "Let's get back to the store."

When they got there, the lady was very nice to them.

"I'm happy you came back here. Mr. Hall was not nice to work for. But I like pets. Now I can take care of them. He didn't care about them," she said. "Is there anything you boys would like?"

"Well," Ricky said, "we would like some turtles."

"Here," she said. "Please take these. You don't have to pay for them. These are the same ones you got before. But these don't have any rubies in them."

They all laughed.

When they got back home, they put the turtles back in the rock garden. The turtles seemed happy to be back in the water.

"Let's get plain turtles next time," Tom said.

"I agree," Ricky said.

Even Patches barked and wagged his tail.

"Please take these. But these don't have any rubies in them."